Whale Port
A History of Tuckanucket

Illustrated by Gerald Foster
Written by Mark Foster

HOUGHTON MIFFLIN COMPANY BOSTON 2007

Walter Lorraine Books

Walter Lorraine *wⁿ* Books

www.houghtonmifflinbooks.com

Library of Congress Cataloging-in-Publication Data
Foster, Mark.
  Whale port : a history of Tuckanucket / by Mark Foster ;
illustrated by Gerald L. Foster.
    p. cm.
  ISBN-13: 978-0-618-54722-7
  ISBN-10: 0-618-54722-3
  1. Whaling—New England—History—Juvenile literature.
  2. City and town life—New England—History—Juvenile
    literature. I. Title.
  SH383.2.F67 2007
  338.3'720974—dc22   2006018772

Manufactured in China
WKT 10 9 8 7 6 5 4 3 2 1

In 1683, a group of English colonists decided to settle in southern New England. Among them were Zachariah and Mehitable Taber. Late that spring, the colonists landed at a sheltered harbor in a place the native Wampanoags called "Tuckanucket."

WAMPANOAG
VILLAGE

cutting in a
drift whale

drying fish

trading sloop
from Boston

4

Taber farm

fishing
sloop

the landing

The Tabers and other colonists cleared the dark earth of Tuckanucket for farming and pasturing livestock. The waterways and ancient forest provided timber, fish, and game, and the sandy shore offered a good landing for boats. The colonists traded lumber and furs for things from England they couldn't make themselves, such as cloth and iron tools. But there was one resource they had not expected—whales, which occasionally drifted ashore. Whales were valuable. In England, oil from the whale's layer of fat, or blubber, was burned in lamps to provide light. Baleen, or whalebone, from the whale's mouth was used in many ways, especially in clothes. When a whale washed ashore, the colonists quickly saved the oil and whalebone for trade.

The colonists soon realized, however, that only a few drift whales came ashore each year. To get more oil and whalebone, the colonists needed more whales. So fishermen began to hunt the slowest whale, the right whale, in boats from shore. When the whales appeared each winter, Zachariah Taber, his son Jabez, and other men went with their Wampanoag neighbors to shore camps. There they helped harpoon whales, cut blubber, and tend the bubbling cauldrons of oil. It was hard, dangerous work, but the valuable whale made it worth it.

camp

a capstan pulls the whale

whaleboats

tryworks

The right whale was so called because it was the "right" one to hunt: averaging fifty feet, it was slow, floated when dead, and yielded one hundred or more barrels of oil and 1,500 pounds of whalebone up to eight feet long.

Right whales migrated along the coast in winter, filtering food from the ocean with their seivelike baleen. Whale fishermen built camps where they passed near shore, with a hut for each boat crew and a lookout. Native men were hired as rowers and harpooners. When a whale was spotted, boats were launched through the surf.

Whales were towed to shore and the blubber was cut away, then boiled to remove the oil. Boiling was "trying," the huge cauldron a "trypot," and, set in brick, the structure was a "tryworks." Shore settlements from Cape Cod to Delaware Bay, with native help, depended on the right whale and shore whaling.

When Zachariah and Jabez were away, Mehitable and the children took care of the farm, from cooking and caring for the animals to chopping wood. Their house had one large room where the family worked, washed, cooked, and ate. There was no toilet—the family went outdoors or used a chamber pot. For many years, shore whaling helped pay for the few tools and clothes they had . . . until one season when there weren't very many whales.

ONE-ROOM HOUSE

chamber pot

trading oil for tools and cloth

The colonists slept on mattresses of straw, the adults on the first floor on rope beds and the children in the loft. Most food was cooked as a stew in pots hung in the giant fireplace. To clear the land, the colonists killed trees by removing the bark, then planted native corn, squash, and beans between the trunks as the natives taught them. On the south side of their homes, they planted a garden with onions, carrots, and other crops from home. Nearby, they planted orchards and built barns for their cows and oxen—pigs were allowed to run free.

trading sloop

whaling sloop at anchor,
waiting to unload

When whales became scarce at the shore, people thought the fishermen
had scared them away. They worried, for they had come to depend on
the whales. Jabez Taber, however, knew that fishermen at other settlements were building small ships to follow the whales along the coast.
He also knew the fishermen would need a good harbor for those ships.
In the spring of 1725, Jabez told his neighbors that Tuckanucket's
future was not on the farm, but on the sea. He suggested they invite
these fishermen to Tuckanucket. His neighbors agreed.

1725

smith   cooper   tryhouse

building a wharf

whaling sloop unloading casks
of blubber at the landing

trading schooner blown
on shore in a gale

The first to accept was Capt. Thadeus Coffin.
Jabez gave Captain Coffin land in exchange for a
share in his whaling voyages, and together they
built a tryhouse on the shore to boil blubber.
Other fishermen followed. Soon, a little village
began to appear on the banks of the harbor.

Jabez knew there were particular things the whale fishermen would need, so he asked craftsmen who could make those things to come to Tuckanucket. Thomas Conklin, a cooper, arrived that fall and built a shop on Water Street, near the landing. Mr. Conklin made all sorts of buckets, barrels, and casks, but his most important work was making the casks that would hold whale oil.

shook

cooper raising
up a cask

apprentice shaping
a stave on the plane

firing

hooping

heading

Oil casks were made of white oak. With ax, drawknives, and planes, oak was split, cut, and shaped into staves and headboards. Staves were "raised up" within wood hoops, softened by steam and heat ("firing"), flipped, drawn together with windlass and truss hoops, and hooped with iron or wood. Headboards were added with flag (reeds) between to prevent leaks. The parts might be keyed, disassembled, and bundled as a "shook" for later assembly on the ship.

Elnathan Cook, a shipsmith, built his shop next door. Like all village smiths, he made everything from hinges to horseshoes, but whaling equipment and ironwork for ships were his specialties. Neighbors soon heard the ringing of his hammer as Mr. Cook shaped the red-hot iron into harpoons and other tools for the fishermen.

bellows

apprentice

shipsmith

Blacksmiths who specialized in "shipwork" were called shipsmiths. At the glowing coals of the forge, the smith heated iron until it was malleable, then shaped it with the hammer at the anvil. He made many things for vessels, such as bolts, rings, chains, and even anchors. In whaling ports, shipsmiths also made "whalecraft"—whaling tools, including harpoons, lances, cutting spades, and other implements.

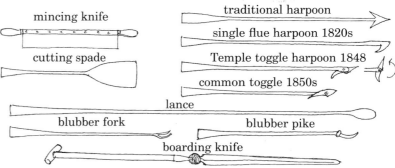

mincing knife

cutting spade

traditional harpoon

single flue harpoon 1820s

Temple toggle harpoon 1848

common toggle 1850s

lance

blubber fork

blubber pike

boarding knife

At first the whale fishermen were successful, but right whales soon became scarce along the coast, too. So fishermen began to venture out to sea—where they found the sperm whale. Unlike common whale oil, which smelled like fish, the oil from this whale, called sperm oil, burned brightly with little smoke or smell, and did not thicken in lamps in the cold. Candlemakers discovered that the mysterious substance in the whale's head, called spermaceti, could be made into sweet-smelling candles that burned brighter and longer than common candles of tallow, or animal fat. But to catch this valuable and dangerous deep-water whale, the Tabers and others had to send their ships far across the unknown ocean.

1720 Small sloops with one or two whaleboats sail the coast for a few weeks for right whales. They tow the whale home or cut the blubber on the shore and bring it back in casks to try out.

1740s Large sloops, with two boats and thirteen men, sail for six months to the North Atlantic in summer for right whales and Mid-Atlantic in winter for sperm whales. They travel in pairs for safety and set up tryworks on a convenient shore to try blubber.

1760s Schooners, with three boats and twenty-four men, sail to the Caribbean and the coasts of South America and Africa for sperm and right whales. Tryworks are adapted to the deck so vessels can stay at sea a year or more.

A toothed whale sixty to a hundred feet long and yielding up to a hundred barrels of oil, the sperm whale lived far from land, where it dove to great depths to feed on giant squid. Sperm oil, from its blubber, made a fine lamp oil. Spermaceti, from a chamber in the head called the case, made the finest candles. Ambergris, a valuable substance used in perfume, was sometimes found in the gut, having formed around the indigestable beaks of squid.

One morning in the autumn of 1758, Lydia Taber anxiously woke her husband, Jabez. The clouds above were dark and the huge ocean swell ominous. By noon, a whistling wind tore shingles from roofs, knocked down chimneys, and uprooted trees. The tide rose into the village, carrying ships and shops with it. When it receded, most of the waterfront was gone. Residents called it the "Great Gale"—the worst storm in Tuckanucket history.

Tuckanucket
Beacon

returning whaling
schooner

Taber's Wharf

Despite the dangers of weather and whaling, by 1770 Jabez Taber's vision had come true. Jabez looked with satisfaction on the homes, shops, and storehouses lining Water Street and to the busy wharves where whaleships unloaded oil. It was Tuckanucket's own vessels that now carried that oil across the Atlantic to light the foggy streets of London. Old Jabez himself had become a successful whaling merchant, trading oil and owning ships with his son Obadiah. The whale fishery of New England, employing three hundred vessels and four thousand men, had become one of the most important industries in the northern colonies. Its success turned the scattered settlement into a bustling colonial port.

1770

storehouse

candleworks   storehouse

TABOR & SON · OIL · CANDLES

whaling schooner taking
on supplies

Though the whalemen brought in the spermaceti, the refining of it remained a secret kept by the spermaceti candlemakers, and they profited by turning it into candles. Finally, after a long search, Jabez's son Obadiah persuaded the foreman of a Rhode Island works, John Chafing, to come to Tuckanucket. With his help, the Tabers opened the port's first spermaceti candleworks. Soon they were trading candles to the West Indies and the "strained oil," a superior lamp oil, to Philadelphia.

oil shed

slack presses

boiler

strainer

molds

candle-making

taught press

shaving

oil refining was a smelly business

Refining separated spermaceti from its oil, with which it was mixed in crude form. In the cask it thickened, so it was first strained, then boiled to remove water and other impurities, and put in casks to cool. The thick oil was then shoveled into bags and pressed between wood plates in the "slack press," a wood screw press, which squeezed out two-thirds of the oil. The spermaceti left in the bags was boiled again and poured into block molds, where it hardened as it cooled. The blocks were shaved

down, folded in cloth, and pressed between iron plates in a "taught press," a powerful iron screw press, removing the last of the oil. What remained was boiled with potash to whiten it and poured into block molds. It was now refined spermaceti. Candlemakers would melt it, then ladle it into candle molds. Once cool, the candles were removed, wrapped in paper, and boxed for shipping. The valuable strained oil was stored in casks, ready to be shipped.

As the town grew, shops appeared. Huldah Tilton, whose husband was a whaling captain, opened a shop in her front room to sell fancy English cloth. Once a year she went with other women shopkeepers to trade oil for cloth in Boston. She also took in sailors as boarders and helped her daughters spin candlewick for the candleworks. Huldah Tilton's house was a home—and a business.

SALTBOX HOUSE

store

kitchen

emptying chamber pots

outhouse

The prosperity in whaling ports brought opportunities. Many homes included shops, often run by women, and offered room and board to sailors. Because whalemen were gone for long periods, women often received advances on their husband's pay, represented him in business, and managed family finances. And to keep from being lonely, they often went visiting.

17

In 1775, war broke out between the colonies and England. Against the wishes of many, several Tuckanucket residents outfitted armed vessels to attack English ships. In September 1779, the English retaliated. The HMS *Badger* landed three hundred troops under General Grudge, with orders to burn the houses, shops, and vessels of suspected revolutionaries. Obadiah Taber, a Quaker opposed to violence, tried to reason with the general. As he did so, local minutemen engaged the English near the town center. Obadiah's efforts were in vain: two minutemen and five English soldiers were killed.

When the English finally retreated, much of Tuckanucket's waterfront was left in flames, including the Tabers' candle-works. But worse followed. After the war, the English refused to buy oil or candles from the new United States. Then came the War of 1812. With ships lost to the wars and no place to sell its oil, the port was crippled. Many residents left, never to return.

Tuckanucket
Light

ropewalk

African Meeting
House

boat shop

When the wars finally ended in 1815, the residents of the port spent everything and
borrowed more in order to send the last of their whale ships to sea. Walking streets
that had been quiet for years, Obadiah Taber was hopeful as he passed craftsmen
and sailors and shops busy with work. The town was now part of a new nation, one
that was growing quickly and needed oil—to light homes, lighthouses, and streets,
and for a new purpose, to lubricate machinery in its factories. As ships returned
with oil from a new ocean, the Pacific, the people of Tuckanucket were optimistic
that the whale might once again bring prosperity and fame to their little port.

Pope house

oil and candleworks

ship carpenters
making repairs

whaling schooner
unloading oil

work raft

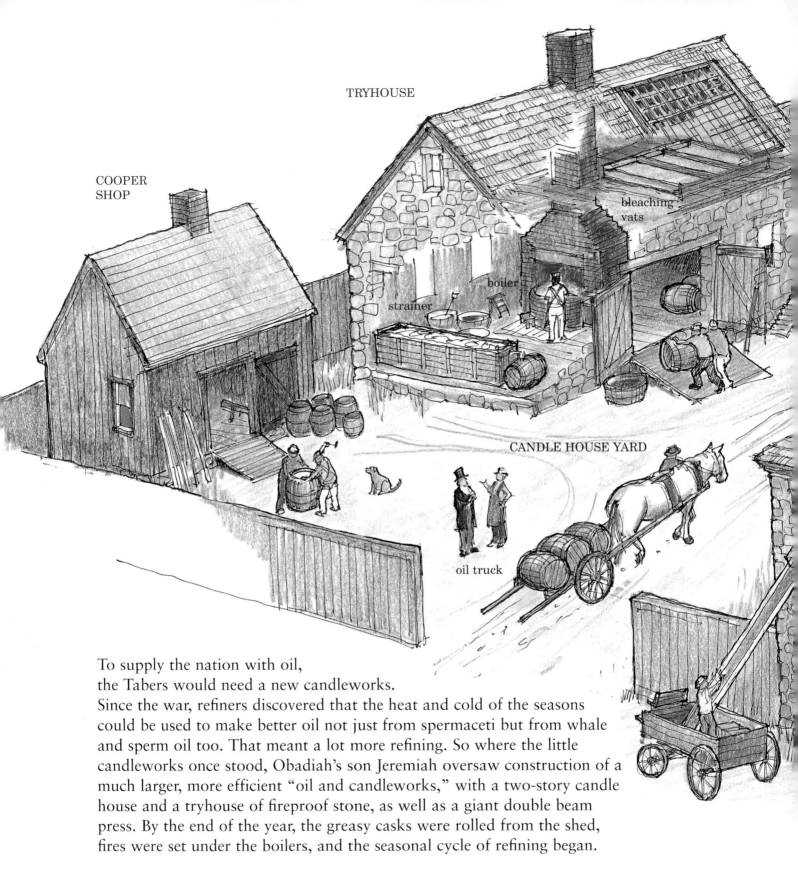

COOPER
SHOP

TRYHOUSE

bleaching
vats

boiler

strainer

CANDLE HOUSE YARD

oil truck

To supply the nation with oil,
the Tabers would need a new candleworks.
Since the war, refiners discovered that the heat and cold of the seasons
could be used to make better oil not just from spermaceti but from whale
and sperm oil too. That meant a lot more refining. So where the little
candleworks once stood, Obadiah's son Jeremiah oversaw construction of a
much larger, more efficient "oil and candleworks," with a two-story candle
house and a tryhouse of fireproof stone, as well as a giant double beam
press. By the end of the year, the greasy casks were rolled from the shed,
fires were set under the boilers, and the seasonal cycle of refining began.

AUTUMN On arrival, all crude oil was boiled in the try-house to remove impurities. Refiners had discovered that spermaceti could be refined from sperm oil too, so now it was mixed with the crude spermaceti. In the fall, all the oil was strained, boiled, and stored in the shed. There, in the deep cold of winter, the oil thickened.

WINTER During a mild spell in January, sperm oil was shoveled into bags and pressed under the giant levers of the beam press. Whale oil was strained through wool or cotton cloth. The result was "winter-strained sperm oil," the finest oil because it remained liquid in lamps in the coldest weather, and "winter-strained whale oil," a similar but lesser grade of oil. What remained was boiled, then stored.

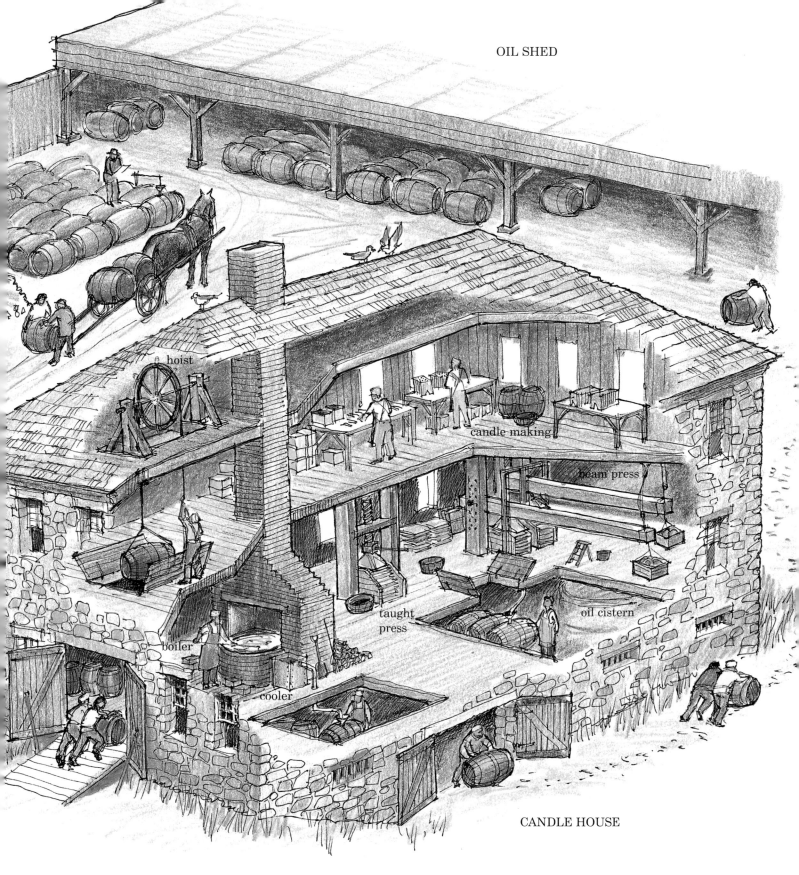

OIL SHED

hoist

candle making

beam press

boiler

taught press

oil cistern

cooler

CANDLE HOUSE

SPRING On a mild day in April, all the oil was pressed in the beam press to produce "spring-strained" sperm and whale oil. Because they thickened in the cold, they could be used only in mild weather. What remained of the whale oil, called "whale foots," was sold to soap makers. The remaining sperm oil, hard and cakelike, went to the shed.

SUMMER In July, the last of the sperm oil was boiled and poured into molds. On a hot day, the blocks were shaved and pressed in the taught press to produce "summer-strained" sperm oil, the least valuable, as it was fluid only in summer. What remained in the bags was boiled with potash, then water. It was now ready to be made into the world's finest candles.

As whale ships returned to sea, opportunities were created for John Cuffee and others. Mr. Cuffee, a boat builder, was a former slave from Virginia and a founder of Tuckanucket's African Meeting House. He purchased an old shop where he, with his son Freeborn, made all kinds of boats, but his specialty was the light, maneuverable whaleboats for the whaling fleet.

steam box

trap

master boat builder

apprentice

Whaleboats were made of white cedar planks over white oak frames. A steam box made the planking flexible for fitting and frames soft for bending in the bending frame, or trap. When a boat was finished, it was painted, then delivered on a special wagon.

assembling keel, stems, and molds

planking over molds

fitting and nailing frames

finishing and painting

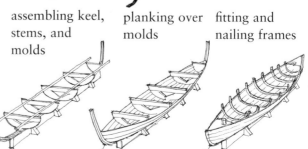

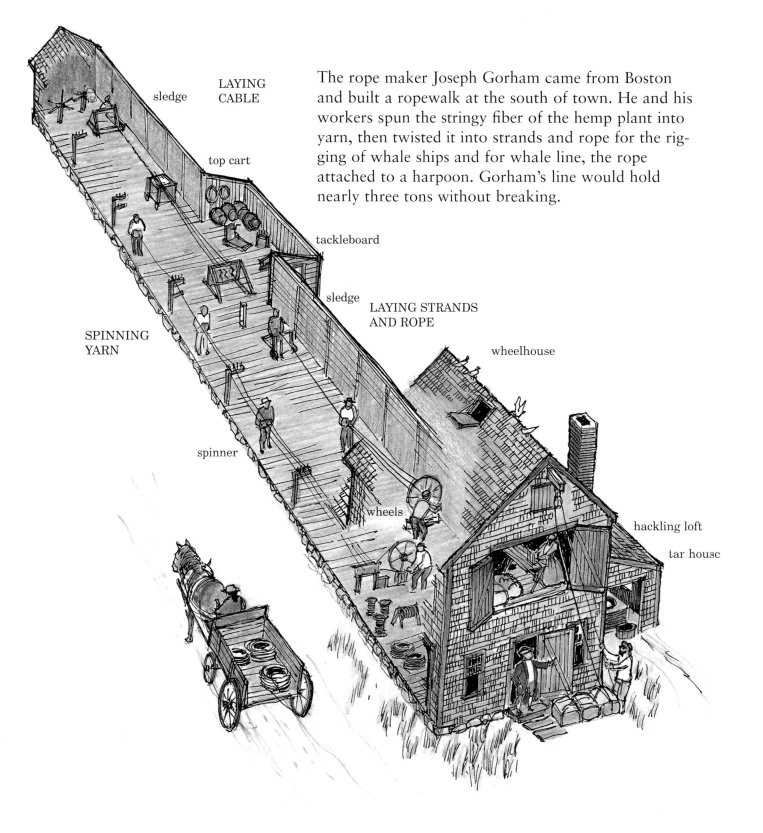

sledge

LAYING CABLE

top cart

tackleboard

sledge

LAYING STRANDS AND ROPE

SPINNING YARN

spinner

wheelhouse

wheels

hackling loft

tar house

The rope maker Joseph Gorham came from Boston and built a ropewalk at the south of town. He and his workers spun the stringy fiber of the hemp plant into yarn, then twisted it into strands and rope for the rigging of whale ships and for whale line, the rope attached to a harpoon. Gorham's line would hold nearly three tons without breaking.

In the hackling loft, women and children used comb-like hackles to draw out the hemp fiber. In the walk below, a man called a spinner gathered a hank of hemp and hung a loop of it on a "whirl hook" turned by the spinning wheel. As he walked backwards, feeding out fiber, the revolving hook twisted it into yarn. The yarns were hung on several whirl hooks and, with a fixed hook at the far end, twisted together (opposite their original twist so they didn't unravel) to form a strand. Strands, fixed to a "sledge" at one end, which kept tension as it was pulled up the walk, were twisted together with an opposite twist to form rope. Ropes, with one end attached to a sledge, were attached to the hooks of a tackleboard, which, when turned, twisted them together, guided by a topcart, to form cable. To make rope more durable, it could be tarred in the tar house.

Lavinia Pope was a seamstress. She sewed sailors' clothes for the outfitter, Mr. Hazard, who sold them to whalemen. Her daughter kept school in their front room. Mrs. Pope supported the family, for her husband, a whaleman, had been lost at sea.

COASTAL QUAKER
HOUSE

summer kitchen with a
small, efficient fireplace

Men who came to ship out on long whaling voyages needed many things, including clothes. Outfitters paid women by the piece for "piecework," clothing made from fabric provided by the outfitter, which they sold to sailors. Teaching was common for single women or widows. And because whaling and the sea were dangerous, there were many widows in the whaling ports.

Sperm oil was used to light mines and in making rope.

The prosperity that returned to Tuckanucket was no accident. Oil from whales was the best oil available, especially for lighting and lubrication. As the country grew, demand for that oil grew with it, for each year there were more people and more businesses that needed more oil. And as more oil became available, people found more uses for it. Wherever the people of Tuckanucket looked, they found something made from a whale.

In the home, sperm oil and spermaceti candles provided light. Sperm oil lubricated fine mechanisms like those of clocks, watches, and guns. Spermaceti was used for hair grease, and ambergris, from the gut of the sperm whale, was used in perfume. Whale oil was used in paint and laundry soap. Spermaceti in the laundry gave clothes a shine.

In public places, sperm oil and candles lit theaters, government buildings, banquets, balls, churches, and temples.

In transportation, sperm oil lit trains, ships, lighthouses, coaches, and streetlights.

In industry, oil from whales reduced the friction that wore out machinery. Whale oil lubricated axles and heavy machinery. Sperm oil lubricated fine machinery like sewing machines and spindles in cotton mills. Sperm oil was also used in finishing leather. And those were only some of the uses of the whale. There were many, many more.

But prosperity could have a price. Fire was always a worry in the fast-growing whaling ports, where wood buildings crowded narrow streets and flammable oil was stored everywhere. On a June night in 1838, Jeremiah and Hepsabeth Taber awoke to cries of "Fire!" It began in a blockmaker's shop, but an argument between the volunteer fire companies allowed it to spread. A brisk wind carried embers across roofs and burning oil soon stretched across the harbor. By the time it was brought under control, much of the town was lost. Residents called it the "Great Fire."

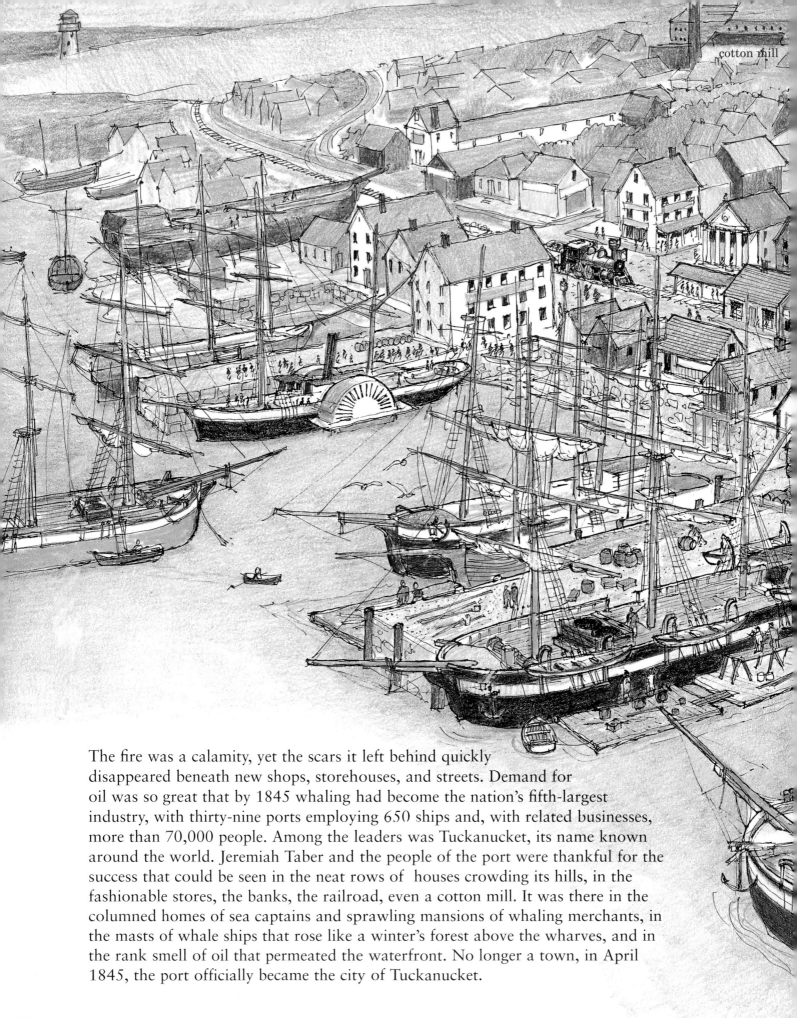

cotton mill

The fire was a calamity, yet the scars it left behind quickly
disappeared beneath new shops, storehouses, and streets. Demand for
oil was so great that by 1845 whaling had become the nation's fifth-largest
industry, with thirty-nine ports employing 650 ships and, with related businesses,
more than 70,000 people. Among the leaders was Tuckanucket, its name known
around the world. Jeremiah Taber and the people of the port were thankful for the
success that could be seen in the neat rows of houses crowding its hills, in the
fashionable stores, the banks, the railroad, even a cotton mill. It was there in the
columned homes of sea captains and sprawling mansions of whaling merchants, in
the masts of whale ships that rose like a winter's forest above the wharves, and in
the rank smell of oil that permeated the waterfront. No longer a town, in April
1845, the port officially became the city of Tuckanucket.

city hall

captains row

1845

Thompson house

SAIL LOFT

CHANDLERY

BAKERY

TAVERN

BLOCKS

COOPER

END SLAVERY

TABER & SON · OIL & CANDLE

TABER & SON

COFFIN & CO.

The busiest part of the city was the waterfront, where all the maritime businesses were located. There, along Front and Water streets, were the shops of coopers, spar makers, and others, the merchants' counting houses where oil was bought and sold, the crowded stores of ship chandlers, and rowdy sailors' taverns. There, you never knew who you might meet—wealthy oil merchants in top hats, country boys come to ship out, or whalemen from all the ports of New England and as far away as the British Isles, the Azores, Madeira, Cape Verde, Africa—even Hawaii. The waterfront was the heart of the port.

The caulker used oakum and tar to caulk the seams of ships.

The ship carpenter repaired the hulls, decks, deckhouses, and other parts of ships.

In the spar shop, trees were trimmed and shaved down into masts and spars.

In the riggers' loft, rope and cable were tarred and served with twine for ships' rigging.

The block and pump maker made blocks for ships' rigging and pumps.

The ship carver carved figure-heads, billet heads, name boards, and other fancy woodwork for ships.

The bakery made ships' bread, a hard biscuit, that would last for a four-year voyage.

The tavern provided food, refreshments, and entertainment for sailors.

33

The most important part of the waterfront was the wharves—that's where the port city met the sea. The busiest wharf was Taber's Wharf, where the whale ships of Taber & Son were loaded, unloaded, outfitted, and repaired. Walking there in the summer of 1845, Jeremiah Taber listened with satisfaction to the hollow knock of caulkers' mallets, the sawing of ship carpenters, the shouts of stevedores rolling casks of oil, and the calling of riggers working high among the masts and spars of his newest vessel, the *Annie Taber.*

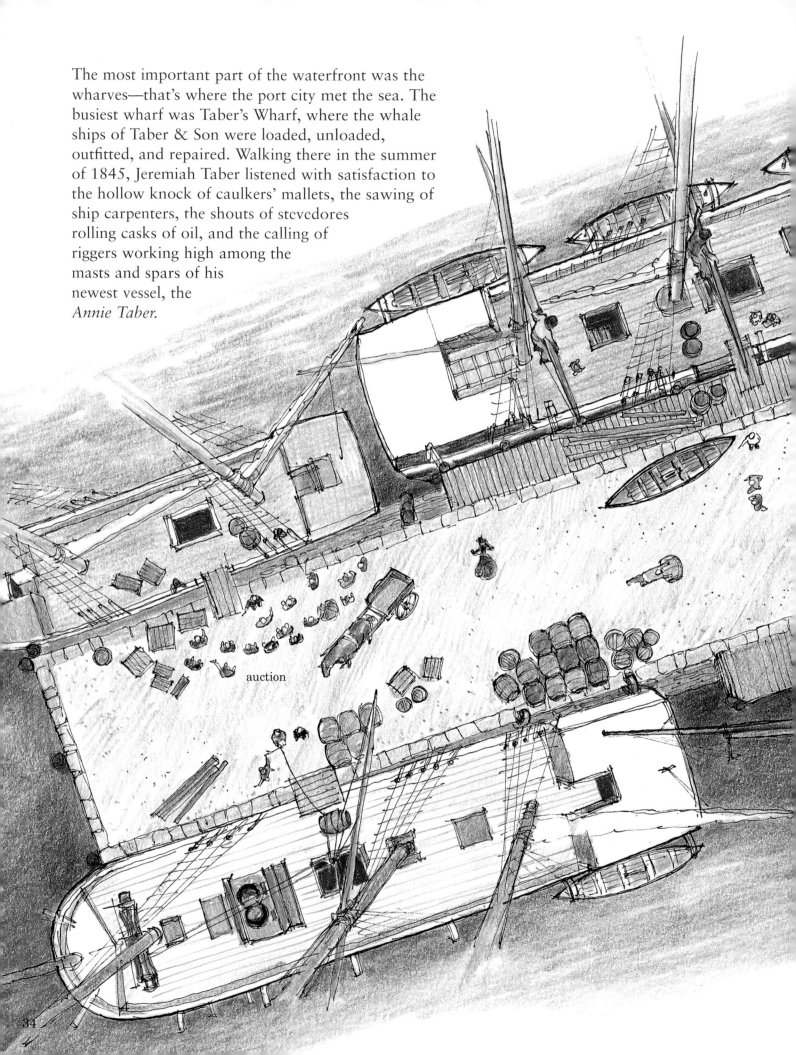

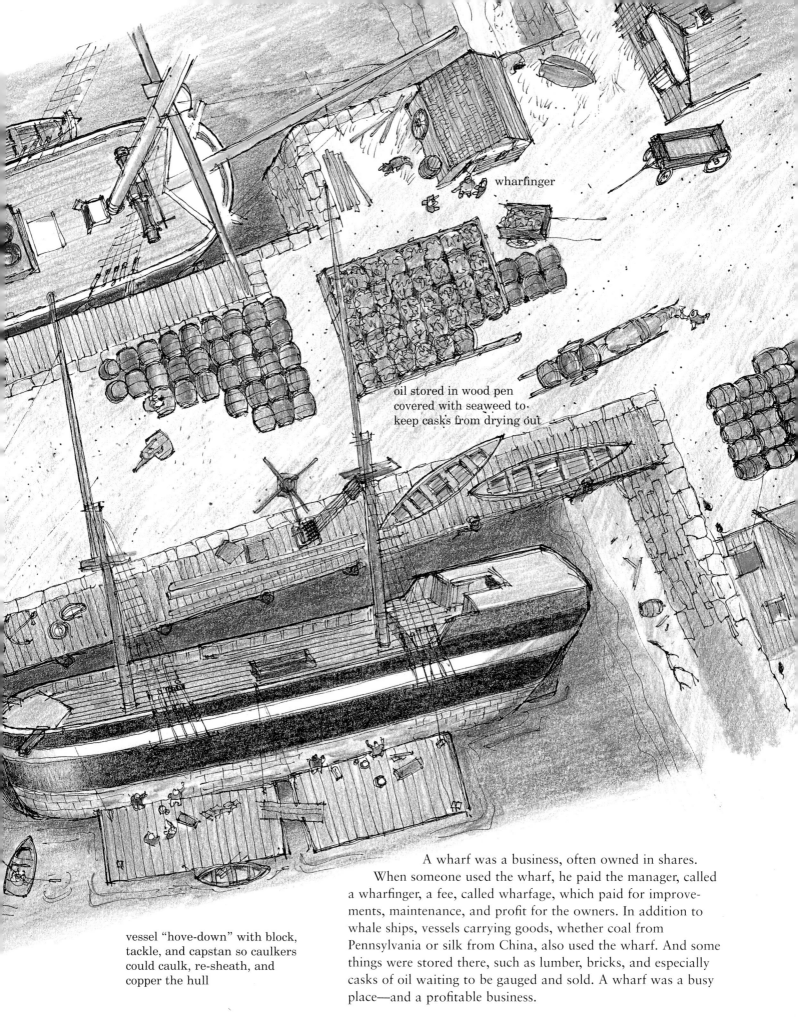

wharfinger

oil stored in wood pen
covered with seaweed to
keep casks from drying out

vessel "hove-down" with block,
tackle, and capstan so caulkers
could caulk, re-sheath, and
copper the hull

A wharf was a business, often owned in shares.
When someone used the wharf, he paid the manager, called
a wharfinger, a fee, called wharfage, which paid for improve-
ments, maintenance, and profit for the owners. In addition to
whale ships, vessels carrying goods, whether coal from
Pennsylvania or silk from China, also used the wharf. And some
things were stored there, such as lumber, bricks, and especially
casks of oil waiting to be gauged and sold. A wharf was a busy
place—and a profitable business.

Jeremiah Taber and other merchants managed their business from counting rooms in their counting house. Jeremiah let his top floor to Mr. Buddington, the sail maker making the *Annie Taber*'s sails, and first floor to Mr. Hazard, the chandler and outfitter recruiting her crew. When Mr. Hazard found a recruit, he brought him to Jeremiah, who looked him over, asked a few questions, and had him sign the "ship's articles," committing him to the voyage and a lay, or share, of the profits.

outfitter
recruiting a greenhand

Top floors were best for sail lofts, for no columns interrupted the spread of sail. Men outlined sails in chalk, marked the outline and depth with prickers and twine, then rolled out the long, narrow bolts of canvas. Each was cut and pegged, then the men began sewing, sewing, sewing.

Whaling merchants owned vessels, bought and sold oil, and acted as ship's agents—managing a voyage by buying, outfitting, and provisioning a vessel, and signing captain and crew. Clerks kept track of all this in ledgers, surrounded by shipping papers, logbooks, and charts.

The outfitter sold outfits (a sea chest with clothes and other essentials), recruited crews, and gave them an advance on their share—and made sure none ran away with it. A ship chandler sold all sorts of things a ship might need, from lanterns and guns to logbooks.

GREEK REVIVAL
HOUSE

While a crew waited to sail, Mr. Hazard sent them to boarding houses like Polly Thompson's. Mrs. Thompson provided a room, meals, and a bed—which might be shared if the house was crowded. Laundry was extra. But Polly took in more than sailors. She and her husband were also abolitionists, opposed to slavery, and often offered their boarding house to fugitive slaves from the South.

efficient iron
cook stove

Boarding houses, often run by women, were essential in ports because they gave sailors, whose homes were often far away, a place to stay. The whaling ports were also a popular destination for slaves because shipping connections with the South provided a means of escape, there were African American communities there, and many other residents were Quakers who were opposed to slavery. Once at a whaling port, fugitive slaves knew they would not be sent back.

By 1845, sperm whales had become scarce and wary in many places, so vessels like the *Annie Taber* were built and outfitted to hunt whales around the world. The *Annie* would be home to her crew of twenty-eight, and the captain's wife, for four years, stopping only for repairs, fresh food, and water. With a rousing shanty, the crew raised her anchor in September 1845. By May the following year, Captain Allen had taken her around the Horn and was cruising north of Hawaii when the man at the masthead yelled, *"Blowwws!"* Every man jumped from what he was doing and ran to lower the boats.

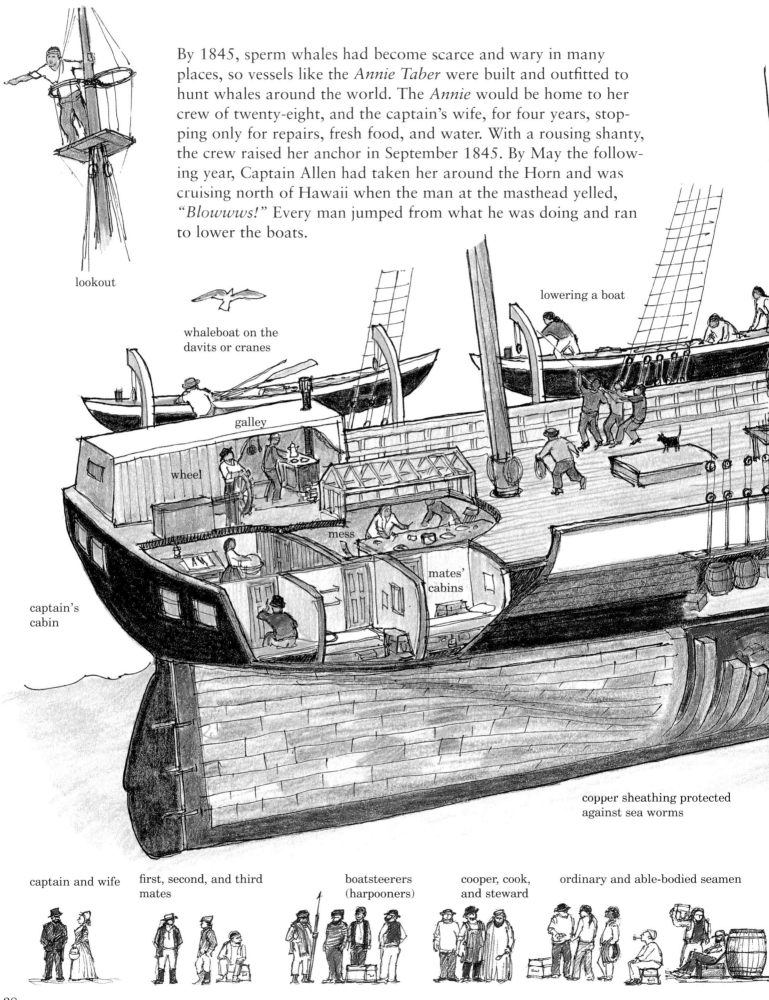

lookout

whaleboat on the davits or cranes

lowering a boat

galley

wheel

mess

mates' cabins

captain's cabin

copper sheathing protected against sea worms

captain and wife

first, second, and third mates

boatsteerers (harpooners)

cooper, cook, and steward

ordinary and able-bodied seamen

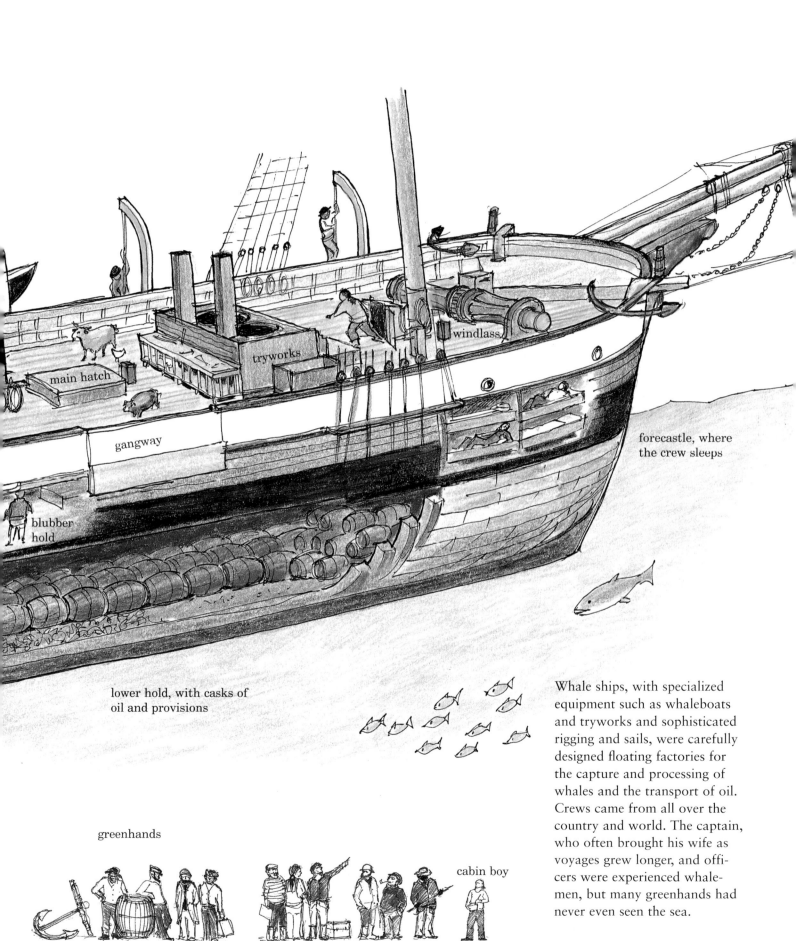

main hatch

tryworks

windlass

gangway

forecastle, where
the crew sleeps

blubber
hold

lower hold, with casks of
oil and provisions

greenhands

cabin boy

Whale ships, with specialized
equipment such as whaleboats
and tryworks and sophisticated
rigging and sails, were carefully
designed floating factories for
the capture and processing of
whales and the transport of oil.
Crews came from all over the
country and world. The captain,
who often brought his wife as
voyages grew longer, and offi-
cers were experienced whalemen, but many greenhands had
never even seen the sea.

Third mate Jorge Cabral was from the Azores. His harpooner, Amos Weeks, was a native of Gay Head. Mr. Cabral had trained his crew well, for they quickly pulled ahead in the race for the whale. As they drew near, Mr. Weeks stood, braced his thigh in the clumsy cleat, and raised his harpoon. When the racing boat was nearly touching the great dark back, Mr. Cabral yelled, "Dart your iron!" With all his strength, Mr. Weeks drove one harpoon, then another, deep into the whale. The harpoons held, but it wasn't until six hours later, after being pulled through the waves, swamped, and nearly thrown into the air, that Mr. Cabral was able to trade places with Mr. Weeks and finally kill the whale with the lance.

The whalemen used harpoons and line to attach the boat to the whale. The boat, with nine hundred pounds of equipment plus crew, then acted as a drag, tiring the whale as it swam, while the men pulled in or let out line as needed. Tradition dictated the officer (or "boatheader") kill the whale, so he and the harpooner traded places (which is why the latter was called a boatsteerer). The whale might dive, drag the boat on a "Nantucket sleigh ride," or attack. When the whale grew tired enough to be approached, the officer used the six-foot lance to reach the heart or lungs. He killed the whale as quickly as possible, not because he was concerned about the whale's pain, but because the wounded whale was so dangerous. Once the whale was dead, the crew began the backbreaking job of towing it to the ship.

With the whale alongside, Captain Allen and the mates began "cutting in." They removed head and jaw, then used razor-sharp cutting spades to peel away the giant strips of blubber, called blanket pieces, while the crew heaved on the windlass to raise the blubber and turn the whale. For twelve hours they worked in shifts, among blubber, blood, and salt water, until all the blubber was aboard.

blubber hook

cutting stage

whaleman's cutting-in diagram of a sperm whale, showing the pattern used to remove the blubber

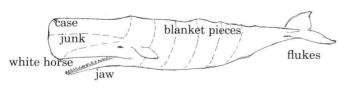

case
junk
blanket pieces
white horse
jaw
flukes

starting the blanket piece, rotating the whale

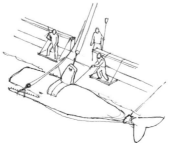

removing the jaw

Then "trying out" began. In the blubber hold, the crew cut the blanket pieces into smaller horse pieces, which were cut at the mincing horse into thinly layered sections called Bible leaves. In shifts, the boatsteerers boiled the Bible leaves, skimmed the boiled scraps to feed the fire, and bailed the hot oil into the cooler. For three greasy days and nights they toiled in the stench of burning blubber and sooty smoke until the all the whale was tried.

bailer

horse pieces

cooler

scraps

mincing Bible leaves

removing the "head" (case and junk)

boarding second blanket piece, lowering first into the hold

separating the case from the junk, carcass set adrift

bailing spermaceti from the case

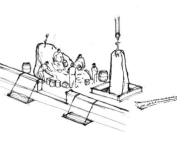

In September 1849, the *Annie Taber* returned to Taber's Wharf, where a crowd of friends, family, and owners greeted her. After four years, she held 1,200 barrels of oil in her hold. With the voyage over, the crew was anxious to get paid. But when the oil was sold, they found that Taber & Son and Captain Allen made a lot of money—while many of the crew made almost none.

The purpose of a whaling voyage was to make money. Profit was divided among owners, who owned a vessel in shares, and captain and crew, who signed on for shares. The ship's agents were usually the largest owners, but they also made money by charging a commission for organizing the voyage, for selling the oil, and for things sailors bought from the ship, for which they charged interest.

A sailor's share varied with experience (averages at right). But out of his share often came his initial advance, outfit, boarding, items purchased from the ship like clothes or tobacco, and cash advances—all with interest. Mates and boatsteerers often did well. Most greenhands never went whaling again.

captain 1/15

first mate 1/24

mates 1/50

cooper 1/60

boat-steerers 1/100

cook, steward 1/160

seamen 1/160

green-hands 1/190

cabin boy 1/400

owners 2/3

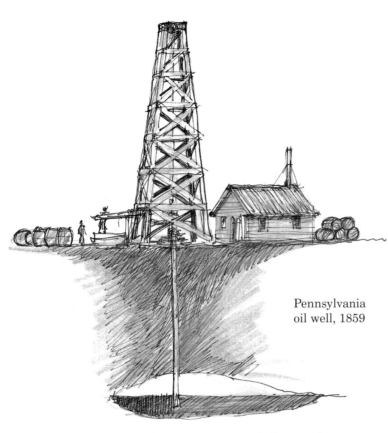

Pennsylvania
oil well, 1859

To many it seemed Tuckanucket's prosperity would never end. But in 1859, Jeremiah Taber read about an Edwin Drake, who had drilled a well in Pennsylvania that produced a thick black oil called petroleum. Petroleum wasn't new, but Drake's well and others produced it easily and in large amounts, which made it cheap. From it, refiners made a bright, clean-burning lamp oil called kerosene. A by-product was paraffin wax, which was made into hard, white, bright-burning candles. Within the year, sales of whale and sperm oil began to fall.

Then, in April 1861, Jeremiah learned war had broken out between the North and South. Many whale ships would be lost to Southern raiders. Others were sunk as part of the Stone Fleet in a failed attempt to block Charleston Harbor. When the war ended, cheap kerosene became the country's favorite oil. Jeremiah took comfort in the preservation of the Union and defeat of slavery, but he feared for the future of Tuckanucket.

right whale
= 100–130 barrels

sperm whale
= 60–100 barrels

bowhead whale
= 100–150 barrels

four-year voyage
= 1,200–1,800 barrels

per day Pennsylvania oil
well, 1862
= 1,500 barrels

1 barrel
= 31.5 gallons

Pennsylvania
oil field, 1860s

whalebone shop

Annie Taber, Captain George Cabral,
refitting for the Atlantic

rigging sails,
bark *Polar Bear,*
in preparation
for the Western
Arctic

As the petroleum industry grew, a
quiet settled over Tuckanucket's
waterfront. Old Jeremiah Taber
watched as grass grew on
empty wharves, shops and
storehouses closed on Front
Street, and old whale
ships that once sailed the
globe were run aground, broken up, and sold for firewood.
People came to the city, but now it was to
work in the mills. To survive, Jeremiah looked for
new uses for oil, mostly to lubricate everything from
bicycles to train axles, and he made the Taber Oil Works more
efficient, adding steam boilers and powerful hydraulic presses. But
oil alone wasn't enough. Hoping the fishery might revive, he and
others looked to an old product: whalebone, for which there was
new demand. Right whales, however, had become scarce. So
Tuckanucket's ships sailed for a new ocean, one that was far away,
cold, and dangerous, in pursuit of a new whale, the bowhead.

1880

Cabral
House

SAILOR

TAVE

TABER & SON

COFFIN & CO

CAUTION!

47

Arctic whale ships had reinforced bows, a bark rig for maneuverability, and partial roofs to protect crews. New "darting guns," with both a toggle harpoon and an exploding bomb, were used to kill the whale. Ships arrived in April, hunted through June, when bowheads disappeared in the pack ice, refitted or hunted walrus in July, then followed the melting ice and bowheads north, retreating ahead of the ice by late September.

blanket piece started, rotating the whale, and headbone chopped free

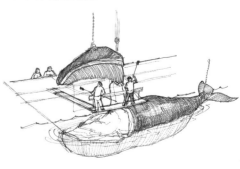

headbone hoisted aboard with the whalebone

headbone   blanket pieces

lip

flukes

With blubber eighteen inches thick, the seventy-foot bowhead could yield three hundred barrels of oil and three thousand pounds of whalebone up to twelve feet long. But its home was the Western Arctic. There, the restless weather might change in a moment, with thick fog and blinding snow squalls, howling winds and rain, and ice that could crush a ship or carry it ashore. In April 1880, Capt. Parnel Spooner and the crew of Taber & Son's bark *Polar Bear* anxiously worked in the wet snow and wind to finish trying out their first bowheads before a rising storm made it impossible.

cut from headbone, the whale-bone is chopped into sections

later, each slab is split from the sections, washed, and scrubbed

then dried in the rigging and on deck, bundled, and stored

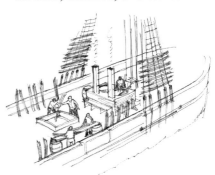

weighing and
sorting

inspecting

washing

drying

Whalebone ware-
houses were often of
stone or brick, with iron
doors, to protect against rats,
which ate the bone. There, whalebone was inspected, washed, dried
outdoors in stands, then graded, sorted,
weighed, and bundled for shipment.
Because San Francsico was close to the Arctic,
it quickly became the leading whaling port.

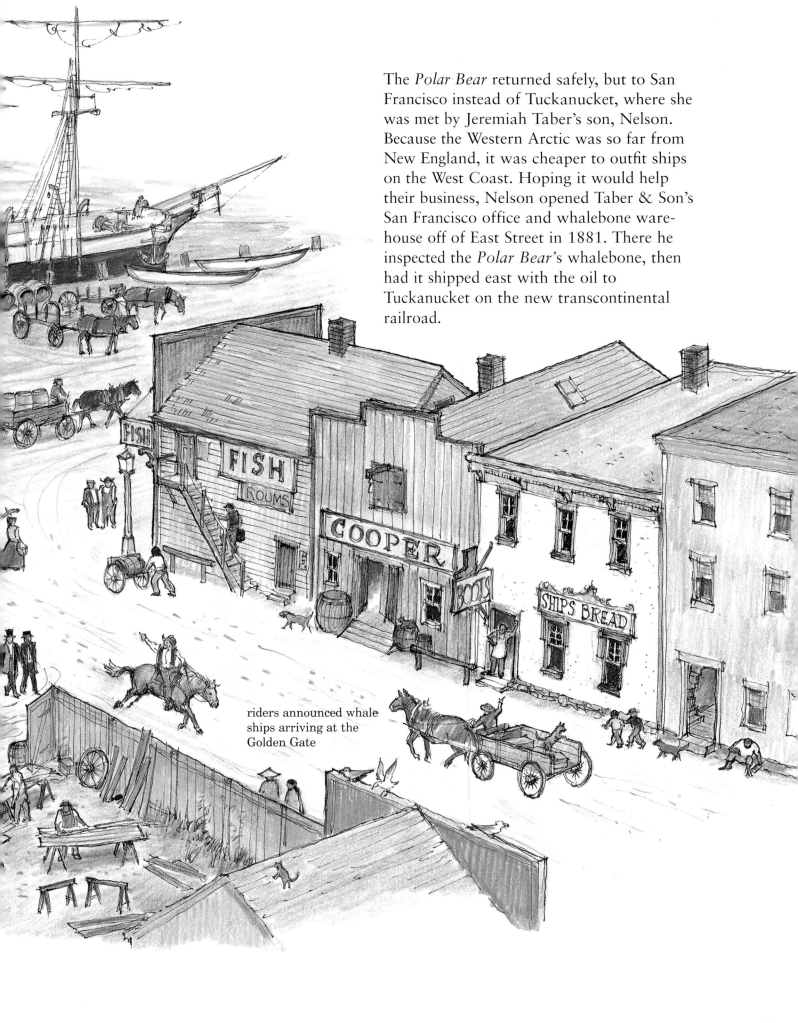

The *Polar Bear* returned safely, but to San Francisco instead of Tuckanucket, where she was met by Jeremiah Taber's son, Nelson. Because the Western Arctic was so far from New England, it was cheaper to outfit ships on the West Coast. Hoping it would help their business, Nelson opened Taber & Son's San Francisco office and whalebone warehouse off of East Street in 1881. There he inspected the *Polar Bear*'s whalebone, then had it shipped east with the oil to Tuckanucket on the new transcontinental railroad.

riders announced whale ships arriving at the Golden Gate

The Tabers sold their "bone" to the whalebone manufacturer George Gifford of Tuckanucket. In his shop, skilled workmen called bonecutters used drawknives and splitting machines to cut the huge slabs down to standard sizes. Most would be used in whips or as the support or "boning" in narrow-waisted corsets and dresses that were the current fashion. The *Polar Bear*'s whalebone was soon found in everything from stylish ladies' dresses to the whips of stage-coach drivers.

trimming

CUTTING: Whalebone was trimmed (the fringe sold for brush bristles) and soaked for a week. Then it was softened by steam and cut with the grain into strips of front bone, back bone, and either whip bone for whipmakers or full-length cuts.

SPLITTING: The strips of front bone and full length cuts were steamed, turned on their side, and pulled through a splitting machine to split them into strips of more flexible and valuable exterior shell bone and more fragile interior grain bone.

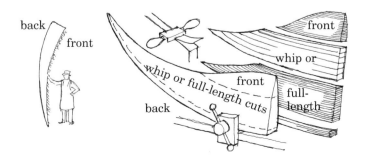

back
front

whip or full-length cuts
back
front
whip or
front
full-length

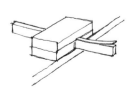

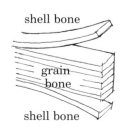

shell bone
grain bone
shell bone

steaming

soaking

cutting

cutting

splitting

packaging

GIFFORD & COMPANY
WHALEBONE MANUFACTURER

OFFICE

DRESS BONE: The flexible shell bone was cut to thirty-six inches, scraped smooth, bundled, and sold to dressmakers as "dress bone."

CORSET BONE: The stiffer grain and back bone was split more narrowly, cut shorter, bundled, and sold to corset makers as "corset bone."

OTHER USES: Because whalebone, like plastic, was flexible and, once steamed, would hold a shape, it had hundreds of uses, from surgical instruments to fishing poles. That's why it was so valuable.

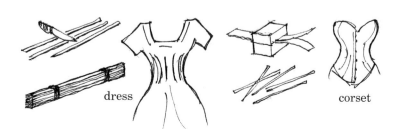

dress

corset

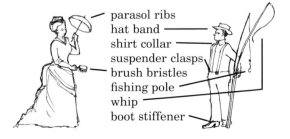

parasol ribs
hat band
shirt collar
suspender clasps
brush bristles
fishing pole
whip
boot stiffener

Even with the demand for whalebone, Tuckanucket's fleet continued to shrink. In the home of Maria Cabral, everyone—Brouchards, O'Malleys, and Cabrals—worked in the mills, except for Maria's grandson Antonio. Antonio loved the sea like his grandfather, Jorge, a whaling captain. But when Antonio sailed on the old *Annie Taber* he found the ship ancient, the work dirty and difficult, and the pay little. When he returned, Maria helped him save his money for a new dream—his own fishing boat.

bathroom

sink

gas stove

TRIPLE-DECKER HOUSE

On a November day in 1919, Tuckanucket's last whaling merchant, Nelson Taber, looked out from his counting house at Tuckanucket's last whale ship, the old *Annie*. The bowhead had become scarce, and its whalebone had been replaced by strong, flexible spring steel. Petroleum had already replaced the whale for lighting and finally for lubrication. When Nelson left at the end of the day, it was for the last time. For Tuckanucket, whaling had ended.

As whaling declined in the United States, in Europe processes were developed to turn the whale into new products—animal food, fertilizer, nitroglycerine for bombs, and fat for use in foods such as margarine. Fast catcher boats with powerful engines and harpoon cannons were developed that could take any whale, not just the bowhead, sperm, or right. They sailed with giant factory ships that could follow the whales into any seas and weather and reduce even the giant blue whale to oil and bonemeal in a few hours. They were so successful, in fact, that they began to run out of whales.

As the years passed, the city turned away
from the sea. The Tabers and other merchants
invested in the mills, and thousands came to work
in them—Irish, English, French Canadians, Portuguese,
and more. But the mills eventually moved south, where
labor was cheaper, and few new businesses replaced them.
Along the waterfront, shops and storehouses were abandoned, rotting wharves
fell into a polluted harbor, and blocks of old buildings were demolished by the
government to make room for a highway that cut the city off from the sea. And
the people of Tuckanucket had other things to worry about—simple things such
as working, getting married, and raising families, as well as two World Wars and
the Great Depression. At Taber's Wharf, only the little fishing fleet remained,
including Antonio Cabral's boat, the *Maria Cabral*.

As the waterfront fell to ruin, residents began to worry that their city and its history were being lost to the wrecking ball, unemployment, and neglect. Some, including Ann Taber, great-granddaughter of Nelson Taber, believed Tuckanucket's residents could change that. For a start, they suggested to their neighbors that they and the city purchase and renovate the old Taber oilworks. Their neighbors agreed.

As people heard of the project, they began to donate things—a harpoon made by Elnathan Cook, the tools of boat builder John Cuffee, Lavinia Pope's sewing kit, a ship's logbook kept by Jorge Cabral, and scrimshaw—the carvings whalemen made from whales' teeth and bone. Two years later, within the old stone walls, a museum opened. There, visitors learned how important the whale had been in the history of the nation and how it helped build a city famous around the world. It was a small start, but it was a start.

A Tuckanucket fisherman, Tony Cabral, was also thinking of the city's past—and future. He often saw whales from his boat and was reminded of his grandfather Antonio, a whaleman. One day, Tony decided to take tourists out see the whales. Before long, so many people wanted to go, Tony had to buy a bigger boat. People called the trip a "whale watch."

WHALEWATCH TOURS
CAPTAIN CABRAL · TUCKANUCKET

MARIA CABRAL IV

endangered North Atlantic
right whale and calf

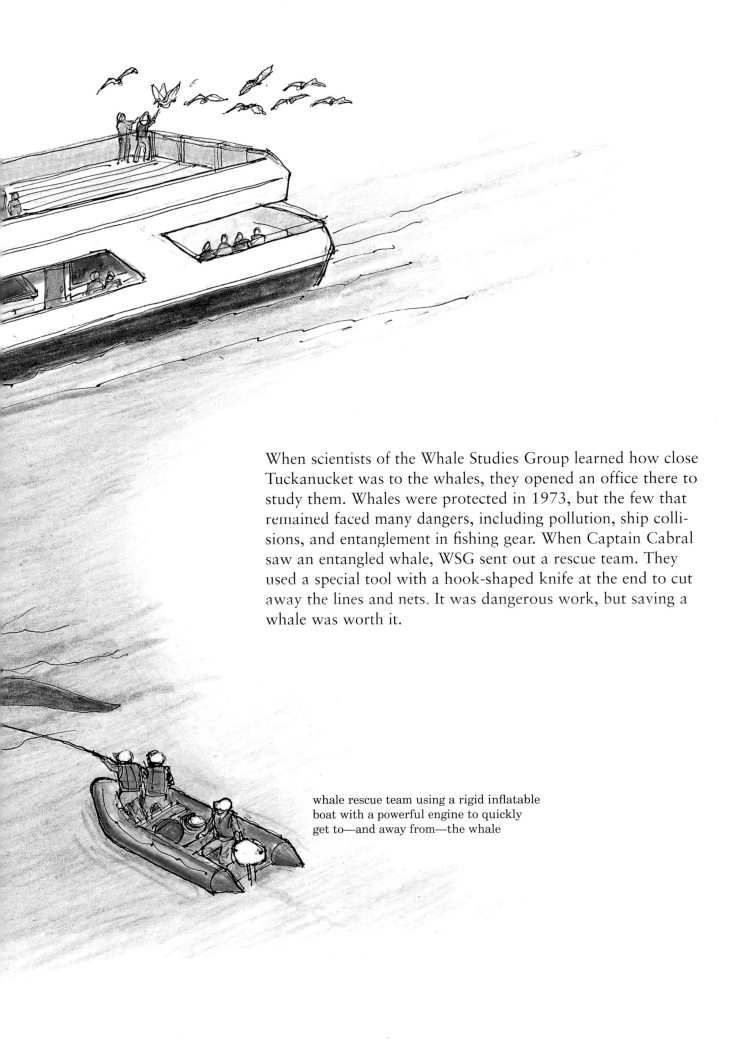

When scientists of the Whale Studies Group learned how close Tuckanucket was to the whales, they opened an office there to study them. Whales were protected in 1973, but the few that remained faced many dangers, including pollution, ship collisions, and entanglement in fishing gear. When Captain Cabral saw an entangled whale, WSG sent out a rescue team. They used a special tool with a hook-shaped knife at the end to cut away the lines and nets. It was dangerous work, but saving a whale was worth it.

whale rescue team using a rigid inflatable boat with a powerful engine to quickly get to—and away from—the whale

With the efforts of its citizens, the old
whaling port began to revive. Ann Taber and
Tony Cabral, the Coffins, Conklins, and Cooks,
the Cuffees, Popes, and Thompsons, and others,
looked with pride on their city. New businesses began to
take space in the old mills, bringing jobs. Along Front Street,
old buildings and wharves were repaired. The pride of the waterfront
was Taber's Wharf, purchased by the city as a permanent home for its
fishing fleet and the stately old *Annie Taber*, restored and resting
alongside. Again people came to the city — to work, see the fishing
boats unload their catch, walk the deck of the *Annie*, and visit the
museum. Strange as it was, they even came to see whales, leaving
daily on Captain Cabral's whale watch to learn about the mysterious
endangered creatures. There was still much hard work to be done,
but it was a new century, and the people of Tuckanucket were optimistic.

A New Century

MUSEUM

WHALE STUDIES

FISH
SEAFOOD

MARINA
CHARTER
BOATS

TRAVEL
ANTIQUES

PUB
LUNCH

BAKERY

ICE CREAM

FOOD

TAFFY

TICKETS

CAPT. CABRAL
WHALE·WATCH

WHALE WATCH

archaeologists
uncover a colonial
shipwreck

Tuckanucket is an imagined place, but its history is shared with other whaling ports, including Nantucket, Edgartown, New Bedford, Fairhaven, New London, Sag Harbor, Provincetown, and many towns of Cape Cod and Long Island. Tuckanucket's tale is one of a whaling port through time, its typical trades, and the diversity of its people. Quakers persecuted in places like Boston settled in several ports. Without Native Americans, early whaling would not have been possible, and they continued to play a role thereafter. By the Revolution, African Americans were a significant presence in the fishery and remained so into the 1850s. Portuguese from the Azores, Madeira, and Cape Verde played an increasing role before the Civil War, and dominated the industry at its end. These people and others from around the world made the ports their home and contributed to the development of their communities. Native peoples of the Pacific and Arctic played important roles in whaling in their areas. The influence of these people and the whale endures in the real ports, as it does in Tuckanucket.

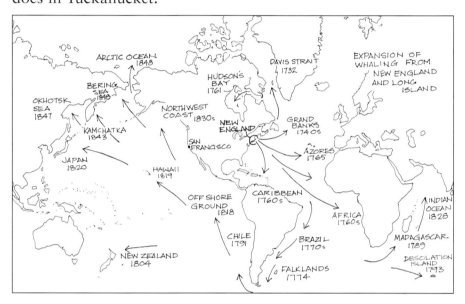

Sources for Tuckanucket include our own research, the Macy and Starbuck histories of Nantucket, Ellis and Ricketson histories of New Bedford, Church's *Whale Ships and Whaling*, and Ashley's *The Yankee Whaler*. More recent work includes Davis et al., *Pursuing Leviathan*, Grover, *Fugitives Gibraltar*, and Norling, *Captain Ahab Had a Wife*. For trades we relied on Horsely's *Tools of the Maritime Trades* and Salaman's *Dictionary of Woodworking Tools*.

This book would not have been possible without the New Bedford Whaling Museum, the Nantucket Historical Association, Mystic Seaport, and the Boston and Concord public libraries. We would also like to thank our friends and family, Concord's Back Alley Cafe, Walter Lorraine, and Erin Wells.

For the problems whales face today, look online for the North Atlantic Right Whale Consortium; the Whale Center of New England, Gloucester, Massachusetts; the Provincetown Center for Coastal Studies, Provincetown, Massachusetts; and the American Cetacean Society, San Pedro, California. For more about Tuckanucket, its making and history, go to www.fosterartandbooks.com.

Index